REASONS WHY WE BROKE UP

REASONS WHY WE BROKE UP

By Laura Ann

OTHER BOOKS BY LAURA ANN

Uncomfortable

PLAYLIST

https://open.spotify.com/playlist/76x92p92GojM1HqZNLi4ae?si=8f47202576c14dc7

TABLE OF CONTENTS

THIS IS FOR HER

To the Emilys who think this story is about them:

You deserve happiness and everything we could never give you.

To the Emilys who hate that I used "Emily":

I'm sorry.

To my Emily

BROKEN PROMISES

S**HE SMELLED LIKE HONEY ON FRESH** pancakes; she was sweet as chocolate on a cheat day.

Three long years, with love going nowhere.

I never promised her a future – she was *fine* with that.

Until she asked, "Why?"

Emily – here are my reasons.

TIME STOPPED

MARRIAGE AND KIDS WERE NEVER on my mind; I didn't want that. Never thought I'd find… ever have the girl of my dreams. But when I met Emily, it was almost as if I was intertwined with love.

We barely knew each other.

Our paths crossed on Mondays and Wednesdays, at exactly 6.10 a.m. She'd come into the office kitchen and set up breakfast for the team; we'd pass pleasantries.

She took the leap first by asking me, "Would you like my number?"

I must've been high on love because I took it, messaging her without hesitation as if she was leaving my life.

Surprisingly, Emily replied to every one of my babbling messages.

A week after she gave me her number, I wanted to

get to know Emily outside of our mornings together and text messages, so I worked up the courage to type, "Do you want to hang out?"

You should've seen how giddy I was when I read, "Sure." I was swept up in the world of love.

"7 p.m. Thursday? Gutter Ball?"

Emily's reply said that she was fine with the idea, and she'd meet me there.

Probably weird for two thirty-year-olds to go bowling, but I wanted to see her smile, notice how competitive she could get, hear her laughter, even notice the little ways she scrunched up her face as the ball hit the gutter.

I was hypnotised by the woman in front of me. It was as if Cupid had hit me with an arrow as she sat down waiting for me to take my fourth turn.

Emily looked beautiful as she picked up her drink. The way she averted her eyes from me; the way she pushed a piece of stray hair from her face…

We hadn't even made it through the first date when my waste of a mouth said, "Emily, I love you."

It was almost as if time had stopped. Maybe she had stopped breathing?

The pit in my stomach felt heavy as Emily opened her mouth. "Thanks."

Maybe we were back to square one.

Driving home left me alone with my thoughts; thoughts of how easily I'd stuffed it all up.

FIRST PROMISE

SURPRISINGLY, EMILY PLAYED OFF my "I love you" as nothing. She explained that no one had ever told her they loved her, and she didn't know how to react.

Maybe she had a damaged upbringing? Maybe her ex-partners were unkind to her?

I promised myself I'd never be that person.

Even though I'd slipped with my words, Emily and I managed. We saw each other at exactly 6.10 a.m. every Monday and Wednesday, then we continued seeing each other every Thursday at exactly 7 p.m.

Emily always found it odd that I noticed time in such detail. She knew what she was getting into when she entered a relationship with a numbers person, though I did promise to keep statistics away from her.

AWKWARD

NEITHER OF US WERE QUITE SURE how it happened, but Emily ended up in my bed three weeks later. We didn't have sex, which was disappointing, but at least I had someone I loved in my blankets.

I wrapped my arm around her as she lay with her back to me. She tried to squirm away from my touch, but I didn't want to let her go, even when she claimed, "It's too hot – do you mind?" She didn't sound mad; just didn't sound like herself.

The night wasn't even hot – it was a cool springtime. Then again, I had layers of blankets on my bed, so I tried to respect her wishes, even though I kept my body close to hers.

Unfortunately, Emily was gone when I woke up in the morning. It would've been nice to see what she looked like first thing. Who wouldn't want to kiss their partner good morning or ask how they'd slept? Though it was nice to know she was an early riser. It meant I didn't have to creep around in the mornings.

CRACKS

Three months after my *love you* slip, I saw Emily's "sweet sanctuary." Her words, not mine.

A house, surprisingly. On twenty acres. Nothing about her had told me she loved this type of lifestyle.

I was too lost in the shock of knowing my sweet little breakfast prepper was an outdoorsy woman. How hadn't I seen it? Who knows?

I could see her lips moving, but I couldn't hear the words she said as she showed me around. It was a four-bedroom house with light-coloured walls, so there were plenty of spaces left to fill, given she lived there alone; there was plenty of space for a second person. It'd be easy for me to help fill those voids.

Her house was peaceful, silent. It almost felt like I could go insane from the sound of my own heartbeat.

But there was a beauty in knowing that Emily had

shared her home with me.

ONE OR TWO?

EMILY WAS ALWAYS HOME BEFORE me. Every time I came home, I used to think that living alone had caused Emily to forget about cooking dinner for two. Then I realised she *never* cooked for me.

Maybe she was selfish?

One night, after a long, stressful day, I snapped, "Why the fuck do you never cook for me?"

The way she startled, almost as if she'd retreated to another world, the way she blinked to stop the tears, the way her lips moved as she tried to form something expressive caused my heart to ache.

"Emily, I'm sorry."

Those genuine words caused a chain to snap cause she crumbled into a mess. She wouldn't even let me touch her that night.

The next morning, she watched me make a coffee

in my travel mug and said, "I don't know how to cook for two."

How could a woman who catered for a living not know how to cook for two?

"Because you always buy takeaway?" I asked, trying to sound casual. I couldn't think of another explanation.

Emily shook her head. "Every time I cook for two, it ends up in the bin. So I don't."

It ends up in the bin. Whoever had hurt Emily before I came along had clearly done a number on her.

"I promise not to throw it in the bin."

The weakest smile appeared across her lips.

I had that weekend off, so I showed Emily how to cook for two – me and her. She was like a child who thought they could do it all, only to flinch at every word I spoke.

It was almost as if she was too scared to show me what she could do. But how could a woman who earned a living preparing food be afraid to touch her own kitchen?

Quiet in Bed

SIX MONTHS INTO OUR relationship, Emily finally allowed me to touch her sexually. It reminded me of the first time we shared her bed – we were just there, though the first time we slept side by side, she'd tried not to create a barrier between us.

Now that we were naked, the experience was uncomfortable. She was quiet, not even a "not that." Or "please stop". I wanted to hear her moan my name; I wanted to know what she sounded like when she came, if she came, but I got nothing.

It almost made me feel like *I* was nothing.

Afterwards, we cuddled, and she laid her head on my chest.

Who dates someone for six months and finds sex with them to be repulsive? It's supposed to be normal. It's supposed to be how a couple shows their love. Six months she'd made me wait. Six months and all I got was a stiff starfish who was scared to make any type of sound.

I was the noise in the room. The one who huffed and puffed, while she just stared up at the ceiling.

ONE YEAR

O**NE YEAR IN, MY LOVE** for Emily had changed; *she* had changed.

Our sleepless nights were perfect now – her screaming out my name, telling me what she liked and how she liked it. It may have taken a year for it to happen, but the wait was worth it. Feeling her tug at my hair when I hit her sweet spot, having her fingernails dig into my ass when she rolls her eyes back, the way she breathes in my ear when I have my lips against her neck, the way her thighs hold my head tight while I eat her out… I treasure every single moment.

On the nights she was home before me, I'd get text messages saying, "I'm cooking dinner – do you want some?"

I would've preferred if she'd automatically made me dinner, but I took what I could. I assumed she was getting used to cooking for two.

On nights I was home at a reasonable time, I'd cook for the two of us, then we'd watch whatever trash kept our attention.

Exactly one year and three days in, Emily finally said, "I love you."

My reply to her was, "Thanks." She looked so confused, I had to remind her what had happened on our first date.

"Emily, I love you."

The pit in my stomach felt heavy as Emily opened her mouth. "Thanks."

She began to explain. "The last guy I was with preferred silence. If he could've silenced me completely, he would've."

In the time I'd known Emily, she'd never once talked about her exes. I'd assumed she had a few, but my ego would've prompted a few questionable words if she'd spoken of them, so I'd never asked. Right now, I let out a slow breath and adopt a sympathetic expression.

And No

IT ALL STARTED AT THE WEDDING of somebody Emily knew. She knows everybody, it seems. How can one person know so many people? I only knew Emily, and my coworkers, and only one of those did I enjoy being with.

Throughout the night, I stayed seated in front of the Emily plus-one name card. She hadn't really introduced me to anyone, even as she smiled, chatted, and danced the night away. We only really stayed together during the meal or when she needed a moment to breathe.

A groomsman asked Emily to dance, and she didn't even look to me to ask if it was okay. Instead, I stayed sitting and watched them slow dance. Seeing his hand on her lower back, the way she rested her head on his shoulder, I was jealous. That should've been me and her. I want to cause a scene but had to remind myself that weddings weren't the place for that.

"Where are all the ladies at?" the DJ wondered. "You know what time it is."

It was almost as if we were in a club given the way the women rushed onto the dance floor, cheering. Emily didn't even look at me as the groomsman left her and she was tugged into the crowd of woman.

She didn't even try to leave as the bride moved in front of the DJ to throw the bouquet.

When I saw Emily catch those flowers, I felt trapped. Like a bat had smashed into my heart – like nothing but emptiness had come crashing through.

I barely registered how excited the ladies were for her as I forced a polite smile onto my face.

Nearly made it to two years…

As with every event Emily took me to, we'd driven to it in *her* car. We never took mine. Why? What was wrong with my car? Sure, it was ten years old and probably needed a new coat of paint, but it got me to and from work every day with minimal issues. Her car wasn't even a car. It was a beast. I had to *climb* into the damn passenger seat, like some stupid baby sitting in a high chair.

The bridal bouquet sat in the middle console.

Stupid flowers – why did she have to catch those stupid flowers?

"I don't want marriage," I said, as if I had a say in something we'd never discussed.

Emily kept her eyes on the dark road. She didn't say anything, but I could see her face each time we passed a streetlight.

My words had hurt her.

Reasons Why We Broke Up

PAIN

THANKS TO MY PAINFUL words, I had to spend the night on the couch as she slept soundly in *her* room. That was Emily's choice – she'd thrown, my pillow on the hallway floor, and kicked my blanket off the bed, than shut the bedroom door in my face.

Who did she think she was? She didn't want to talk about it, the stupid bitch!

Pain II

FTER GETTING USED TO sleeping on the couch in Emily's home, I realised it wasn't that bad. It beat snoozing slumped in an office chair trying to keep the glare of the ceiling lights out of your eyes.

It was almost routine now, waking up alone in her house. But as much as I liked routine, I didn't like waking up alone when I lived with someone.

I'd always thought living with someone you loved would be full of fun, full of butterflies and rainbows, but with Emily, it was all about routine. She liked routine.

I liked numbers, and she liked routine.

The sigh I let out as I sat up on the couch seemed never-ending as I listened to the silence, knowing I had a long day ahead.

I hated that she couldn't talk to me about my thoughts on marriage; I hated that she'd caught the bouquet; I hated that she had to act like she was ready for marriage.

What did she think I was? Just cause I had money didn't mean this was the life I wanted.

She hadn't even bothered to ask me before she joined the partnered ladies on the floor. Why hadn't she just asked me?

We could've solved this real quick if she had.

That's all she had to do.

She could've asked me during the wedding; she could've asked me when the DJ asked for all the ladies on the floor. She could've just asked me. All she had to say was, "Is it okay if I try to catch the flowers?"

But no – she had to be selfish and join all the eager ladies without thinking it through.

She had to be *selfish*!

LOVE OR LOVED?

THE LONG DRIVE TO WORK helped clear my head. It made me realise the idea of marriage was stupid. Who spends a fortune on marrying someone that they'll cheat on a week later?

To say I was grateful I didn't see Emily at work that morning would be an understatement.

I slouched down in my office chair and was able to keep my head focused on the day in front of me… until I needed some air.

God, the breeze on my face felt overly needed. Almost as if I'd been running in the heat, and the moment I'd stood still, my body had soaked in the cool air.

Watching the world around me felt different. It almost felt like I was seeing it for the first time.

This felt different. This felt new.

But I loved Emily. I *loved* Emily. I moved into her

house. I cooked for her. I touched her.

What had Emily done?

Asked to cook for me? Asked me to spend nights at her house?

I couldn't remember if she'd ever even touched me without me starting things first.

Emily

THERE WAS A FEELING IN MY gut as I drove home that night, and I couldn't remember the last time I'd felt it. She hadn't bothered texting to ask if I wanted dinner.

Emily knew I loved her – I'd told her over and over, so how could she not?

That's what couples do, right? They tell each other how they feel confess their love for each other until the end of time.

Yet Emily, never said the words back.

She'd only told me *once* that she loved me.

Whenever I told her – time and time again – she always acted as if she had other thoughts on her mind, so maybe she didn't love me? Maybe she was using me?

I had money. I had privileges that gave me happiness.

All she had was an early morning job.

All she had was a home set in twenty acres of land.

All she had was her life.

I had everything; I'd *given* her everything.

If only she could see how much I did for her.

How could I tell her that she needed to feel the same as me? How could I tell her that this wasn't a one-sided relationship? How could I tell her that this love wasn't for taking, if she wasn't going to give?

Emily – you caused this.

HANGING BY A THREAD

THE DAYS TURNED INTO WEEKS, and still we didn't talk about marriage, but I knew it was constantly on her mind given the way she looked at certain window displays.

It was almost as if I was a toy with which she was playing.

Couldn't she see that I wasn't a toy?

We didn't even talk about kids. But now we had to.

The problem with her and I is our *talks* always came after a moment of pressure. Pressure from friends. Pressure from family. Pressure from TV. Pressure from magazines. Pressure from anything and everyone in *her* life.

Three of her friends had told us they were expecting – they couldn't wait to have their babies be the best of friends. So then, of course, they pestered us with that stupid question: "So? You two? When?"

Seeing the shade of red Emily turned when she was too embarrassed to give a certain answer… Oh, I wanted to squash that colour out of existence.

"First marriage, now kids?" Emily huffed later as she stormed through the house. "What is your problem?"

"Are you serious, Emily? Really? You couldn't have asked me upfront? You just assumed I want both of those? Isn't the whole point of marriage – and kids – that it's a *two-person* discussion, not something you decide on your own?"

"We didn't discuss! You just shut it down. 'I don't want marriage.' And what did you just say in the car? 'If I had children, I'd kill myself.' Who says that? What did you think you were getting into when we started dating? Do I look like the type of person who doesn't want those things?"

Emily seemed to have her life planned, and it didn't involve me.

The silence of my reply could've been heard in space.

"I want to be a wife. I want to be a mother. I want

to spend my days looking back without regret.”

"You'll just end up divorced with a brat." Those words had slipped out without me thinking them through.

That did it.

That caused the rope of our love to snap.

TWO YEARS

O UR TWO-YEAR ANNIVERSARY was coming up.

Neither of us were in the mood to celebrate

HONEYMOON OVER

T HEY SAY WHEN THE HONEYMOON period is over, you start to learn what the person you're dating is truly like.

Emily was like hot air on a summer's day; I was like cold air on a winter's day.

Our love was ~~bliss~~ mismatched.

Two years.

That's how long it took us to understand.

Our second anniversary was spent out in public so we could work through our issues.

Emily wasn't getting any younger, and neither was I. She was still sold on her dreams of being a wife and a mother. I was still staunchly anti-marriage and dreamed of remaining childless.

Two years.

Emily suggested we go to therapy. Why? We were fine.

Who was I kidding? We weren't fine.

We couldn't even talk to each other privately without it turning into a screaming match, yet in public we were the dream couple.

In private, I'd grown used to sleeping on the couch. *Her* couch. You'd think by now I'd be allowed to have my own piece of furniture, especially if I was spending more time on it than her. But no.

In public, I continued to act like she and I had the perfect bedroom habits.

THERAPY

ODAY WAS THE FIRST DAY of what I thought would be couples therapy. Emily had said we needed to go to therapy and work through our problems, but I didn't realise she meant that we had to sort through our problems separately.

Sitting in the waiting room alone, with just the ticking clock and my own thoughts for company, I couldn't help but wonder what my girl was telling this so-called doctor. I needed to know what she was saying about me behind my back; I needed to know everything that Emily couldn't say to my face.

Do you know how many times I thought about barging into Emily's session, to call her out on her cowardice for not talking to me?

When that door opened, my heart almost stopped as Emily walked out, and I was asked to step in.

Emily said, "I'll be back, when you're done."

Like she had anywhere else important to be.

Then it was just me and the so-called doctor, who wanted to know everything about me, while all I wanted to know was what Emily had talked about.

Who knew you couldn't ask what the other had talked about?

The quack had the nerve to ask if I had a temper problem. Why would I have a temper problem? I don't. I raise my voice like any other person on this friggin' planet. I get cranky. I cry. I scream. I throttle pillows. What were they trying to imply? That I strangle my girlfriend? I'm not that twisted!

Then the moron wanted to know about our bedroom habits. So I lied and told the thera*pissed*, "We're just like rabbits – can't keep our hands off each other."

That made the bitch shut up, then of course she had to write it down. Of friggin' course. I'm the one with the issues now, aren't I?

It wasn't like I wanted to be here; this was Emily's choice.

Just like everything else.

It was Emily's choice to give me her number It was Emily's choice that I sleep in the lounge room. It was Emily's choice that I was stuck with a longer commute. It was Emily's choice that made me hate the very sight of my own girlfriend!

It was all Emily's choice!

I was so angry. I was so angry that I felt like I couldn't even look at Emily for the rest of the day.

The tension whenever we were in the same room could be seen from space. It was so thick; it was so disgusting. It was so painful that we both could see the damage this day had done.

THERAPY II

THERAPY WAS THREE TIMES A week. We also had our sessions one after the other – Emily's would be first, then it'd be mine.

Until it wasn't.

The therapist suggested that Emily and I come at different times, and on different days. I have no idea how many times Emily went a week, or even if she went at all.

I did.

At first, I pushed it off – I couldn't go if Emily wasn't with me, right? But then I started going during my lunch break, then started to drift in before work, then sometimes before, during, and after work.

The therapist and I talked through some stuff.

They suggested that maybe I was clingy, needy, and felt the urge to attach myself to people because I'd never got the affection I'd needed from people during my childhood.

Hearing those words hurt like a bitch, and the ugly part of me tried to convince myself not to cry in front of this person who was telling me things I'd never fully understood before. Even though I'd lived through my childhood and knew what I had and hadn't heard, it hurt.

We talked about the first time I'd told Emily I loved her.

"So why'd you say it? You barely knew her," the therapist asked.

That was the truth. We'd talked before my first meeting of the day at work, we'd talked via text message when we'd swapped numbers, but *we'd* never talked about *love*.

I told them I guessed I'd said it because I didn't know the rules when it came to love. I guessed I'd said it because I'd felt *something*, or maybe I thought I'd felt something.

"Do you confuse lust for love?" the therapist asked.

"There's a difference?" I asked.

Turns out there is a difference.

"How many relationships have you been in?"

That question made me pause, holding all my lies back and confronting the truth of it all. The ice-cold truth. The 100% truth that I'd been covering up since I was old enough to talk about sex. It was the one topic I'd avoided being truthful about since meeting Emily.

Emily was my first girlfriend. Emily was my first kiss. Emily was my first sexual experience.

Emily was my first.

I latched on to this woman for all the wrong reasons. I latched on to her because I was lonely; I latched on to her because I felt like I was finally owed this.

I felt owed.

How can a thirty-year-old not be owed? I'd waited patiently for love. I'd done what everyone had said. "You'll know when you're in love."

But how could I know when I'd never been in love?

I'd confused lust for love. I'd confused niceness for love. I'd confused trust for love. I'd confused it all.

I never told Emily about my lack of exes. I never told Emily she was my first. I never told Emily anything about anything.

Maybe that's why she'd suggested we seek therapy apart? Because she didn't have the heart to tell me to my face.

I had destroyed my first and most likely only relationship.

REALISATION

AFTER THAT REALISATION, **I** didn't know what I was supposed to do next. Was I supposed to confess it all to Emily? We never talked about our sessions. We usually let the tension fizzle out on its own.

Was I supposed to confess to Emily that she was my first? Was I supposed to confess that I loved her for all the wrong reasons? That I don't love her the way I probably should?

Was I supposed to undo two years of learning about love all at once?

Was I even fully invested in this relationship?

I lost track of time as I sat in my car, now parked in the driveway. I lost myself to my own thoughts. I lost myself to the truth. I lost myself to everything I wasn't supposed to do.

I lost…

TRUST?

TWO YEARS, ELEVEN MONTHS.

Emily's been acting differently around me.

I found out I'm the only one that's been going to therapy – turns out, she stopped within the first month of our session times changing. Turns out, she only did it to convince me that I needed help.

That was a nice fight.

~~Trust.~~

I still didn't tell her that I couldn't love her.

We constantly fought. We constantly gave each other the silent treatment.

There were no more texts about dinner. No more texts about going to events with her. No more being the plus-one.

Maybe I felt guilty, but who knows?

GHOSTING

EMILY LEFT FOR WORK THIS morning. I didn't tell her what I was doing.

Today was our third anniversary, but the best gift I could give Emily was packing my car – everything I owned all crammed into the piece of crap I've owned for most of my driving life.

I didn't even leave her a note. I didn't even text her. Nothing.

SILENCE

HEALING

I NEVER FORGAVE MYSELF FOR THE way I treated Emily. I never forgave myself for just walking out of her life the way I did.

I continued seeking professional help, working through thirty-plus years of problems I never knew I had until Emily pushed me to seek help.

I learned that it wasn't normal to sleep in the lounge room every single night; I learned that it wasn't normal to move in with someone without a two-sided agreement. Emily wasn't the one who'd pushed me to move in with her; it was me – because I was angry that she never wanted to come over to my place. Look, I still lived at home, so I guess that'd turn anyone off. At first, I'd left a jumper or a lunch container behind, then I eventually just packed what little I had and decorated her house with it.

But if Emily didn't want me living with her, she

should've just said so.

Funny, I blamed Emily for so much during our relationship, but none of it was her fault. Sure, she wasn't a saint, but she wasn't the devil either. She was just the one I loved. Lusted after. Was confused about. She was the woman I used for my own gain.

I think because I was desperate. I was desperate for a cuddle buddy; I was desperate to have someone hold me while I slept; I was desperate for that nightly affection. I was just completely and utterly desperate.

The therapist suggested there had been many signs that Emily wanted me to slow down, but I'd refused to acknowledge any of them.

That wasn't wrong.

Looking through all the text messages between Emily and I, there had indeed been signs. Even looking back at the nights Emily had cooked for me – really thinking about it now, my heart sinks. Her cooking meals for one probably wasn't because of fear but because of me. Had that been her way of telling me she wanted me to leave? Had that been her way of saying she'd never wanted me to move in?

We talked about how Emily had lacked love from her previous partners, but the therapist thought maybe it was just Emily working through her own fears of trust. Of course I had to be the one to push everything to the front of her mind again.

Looking back at our relationship, I'd been afraid the whole time.

Everyone had always told me that I'd know when I was in love. Everyone had always told me that I should've settled down by now, or at least brought someone home by now.

I was living up to what society wanted me to be. What my family wanted me to be. What my friends told me I should have by now.

I liked Emily, but I confused it all.

I confused it all too quickly.

HAPPIER

SHE LOOKED DIFFERENT. She looked happy – full of smiles as I watched her rush around the function room. It was almost as if I was seeing her for the first time as she moved around the crowded room.

The way she talked about the various foods on offer. The way she laughed with a smile. The way she bounced on the balls of her feet. That was the woman I'd once loved. The woman I'd once tried to control. The woman I'd once forced to play by my rules.

Now look at her, catering my work party. Would it be wrong to pray that she doesn't notice me tonight? Pray that I remain just another face in the crowd? I know I took the coward's way out and just ghosted her when I left her house.

My gaze followed her for most of the night, but Emily never once looked at me, never once brought a tray over and described the food on offer.

I hope she is happier now. She looks happier now.

BEGINNING, MIDDLE, AND END

T HERE WAS A LIFE THAT I never thought about before Emily, there was a life I thought about during Emily, and now there's a life after Emily.

I still think about her sometimes. The one I left behind. The one I left with all my burdens; the one I wished I could've loved differently. The one I missed, who I maybe could've been less aggressive with.

Looking back now, Emily was just doing what she thought was right. She pushed me to open my eyes, and I don't blame her.

Why would I blame her?

Emily – I know you'll never read this, but this is my thank you. When I started, I thought this would be the FU to our love, but it isn't.

Emily – I just want you to know that I'm sorry for wasting our time.

Emily – I'm sorry for feeling like I was the more important one in our relationship. I'm sorry for making you feel like you were supposed to play second best to someone who didn't know better – someone who'd never experienced love before. I'm sorry for not telling you the truth. I'm sorry for letting my ego get the better of me. I'm sorry for always saying, "At least I don't hit you." I'm sorry for never listening to you when you said you wanted a fairy-tale love after all the years of heartbreak you'd suffered.

Now that I have all this off my shoulders, I can tell you that I've found a new part of myself.

I've fallen in love, surprisingly. And this time I'm happy with them. They're not you, Emily, but at least our love is *two-sided.*

Laura Ann

ACKNOWLEDGMENTS

Where would this book be without all the people I've ever crushed on? All the times I dreamed of a future with them, only to be either too afraid to tell them that I liked them or have them find out about my crush and have it be turned into the butt of a joke. Fourteen-year-old me still feels haunted by those jokes.

This book came out of a realisation about the way I'd viewed love up until recently; about the pressure society puts on people to find love by a certain age. The trouble is love isn't about forcing yourself to be with someone; it's about allowing things to happen organically and what you both want out of something.

To the last person I crushed on, I'm thankful you turned me down because I needed that chance to explore my own feelings. This book is actually dedicated to you, though you'll never know that because your name isn't actually Emily. It actually starts with "Z", and you don't work in the hospitality industry.

My editors, Sara O and Laura K. I love you both, thank you so much for helping me make my book suitable for readers.

My amazing small team of beta readers, Emilia Dashfire and Laura Christian. This baby author would be no where without you two. Thank you so much for your insight with this book and giving me a readers guidance of how it'd be viewed.

Laura Ann

ABOUT THE AUTHOR

Laura Ann is based in Queensland, Australia. *Reasons why we broke up* is her second book, she's quite excited to be part of this author world and can't wait to show readers what else she has in store. A bonus is her revisiting all the fictional worlds she's created.

Outside of writing, Laura turns her eyes square by sitting too close to the TV and spending too much time immersed in the imagination of others. Laura's also a book hoarder who can't seem to make her TBR pile shrink, even if her read pile lets her believe she's made a dent in it, and a self-taught sewer who frustrates herself by not reading pattern pieces correctly when she's designing her own costumes for cosplay.

If you'd love to follow Laura via social media, she goes by EntrancedbyWords on both TikTok and Instagram.

www.ingramcontent.com/pod-product-compliance
Lightning Source LLC
Chambersburg PA
CBHW021748190726
48290CB00008B/2533